One Mad Apple

by

Tom Pratt

3/30/22

DORRANCE
PUBLISHING CO
EST. 1920
PITTSBURGH, PENNSYLVANIA 15238

Dorrance Publishing Co
585 Alpha Drive
Pittsburgh, PA 15238
Visit our website at www.dorrancebookstore.com

ISBN: 978-1-6480-4117-4
eISBN: 978-1-6470-2619-6

Enjoy the ride and I appreciate your feedback.
Contact me at tompratt973@gmail.com.

This book is dedicated to all past and present school board members. Thank you for your commitment and service to your community. Also, to my Mom and Dad. Without them, this journey would have never happened.

Thanks

This journey began when I signed up for my first writers' conference sponsored by Manzanita Writers Press located in the Sierra Foothills of northern California. This event inspired me to keep writing and pursue my goal of being an author.

The following people encouraged and provided me with invaluable insight and advice: Kristy Billuni (my incredible writing coach), known professionally as The Sexy Grammarian, Sally Kaplan, David Vassar, Ara Thorpes-Billuni, Jerry Billuni, JoEllen Gano, Jenny Baxter, Tom Eising, Terri and Mark Wilson, Kyle Wilson, Sandra Beals Hess, Dennis Billuni, Louise Simson, Mike Miledi, and Mark Hess.

Special thanks to Kirsten Gomez for hosting the first book signing event, my sister, Terry Salazar, my brother and psychological advisor, Steve Pratt, Pati Barton (who read every rewrite and pushed me to finish the book!), and my wife, Kimberly for her unconditional support and love.

Lastly, to my boys Tommy and Hutton. May they realize all their goals and dreams.

Author's Note

This book was written to be a multi-sensory experience. With this in mind, I recommend requesting Amazon's Alexa to play the listed song before or at the end of the chapter as indicated. The lyrics are significant and have a special meaning to the story.

The One Mad Apple playlist is as follows:

CHAPTER 1

New York Minute

(The thump of techno music is playing in the background.) Newly divorced Jake, the owner of a chic, popular art gallery and wine bar in a big city, is pouring a glass of champagne. He walks toward a beautiful and exotic young woman that is very enamored with him. He hands her the glass, smiles, kisses her on the cheek, and walks away to greet all the movie stars, celebrities and beautiful people attending the latest art opening at his gallery. Jake is living the life most of us dream about. He owns a successful wine bar, art gallery and an art insurance investigation business. He loves the high life, attention and living in the big city. This is his element.

While he is negotiating a deal with a movie star ready to buy a painting, his assistant, Bridget, approaches him with a profoundly serious expression on her face. She blurts out, "Jake, there is an urgent telephone call for you." He tries to dismiss it, but Bridget is insistent. Then she finally yells over the music, "Jake, it's your mother, Goddamn it!"

Suddenly, Jake grabs the phone and says, "Hey, Mom, what's up?"

His mother, Margaret, slowly says, "Sweetheart, I can hear in the background you're busy, this can wait."

Jake interrupts his mother by saying, "Mom, please don't do that guilt thing. That worked when I was a teenager, but not now. What's the matter, it must be serious? I always have all the time in the world for you."

What his mother tells him brings an icy-cold shiver from his brain down to his toenails. Margaret speaks slowly and deliberately. "Jake, I have stage four brain cancer and it doesn't look good. I didn't tell you right away because I don't want you to worry, but now I don't know how much longer I have."

Jake wipes the streaming tears down his face, composes himself and speaks softly. "Mom, what can I do to help you and Pop?"

Margaret replies, "Nothing, sweetheart, I just want you to know."

The next day, Jake requests a meeting with his business partners in the wine bar and art gallery. He passionately expresses his mother's condition, his need to sell his interest in the businesses and go home to help his father take care of his mother. Every one of the partners agrees this is the right thing to do, and they draft an agreement to buy out all his shares. Jake is incredibly grateful and breathes a sigh of relief, because his business partners are all so compassionate about his personal situation. He then makes plans to move up to the small rural California community where his parents live.

It is blazing hot the first day Jake arrives in his new hometown. It is 115 degrees in the shade, and the northern half of the Golden State is on fire. A strange orange hue covers the sky.

Jake's eyes and throat burn from the smoke-filled sky. The small house he is renting in his new hometown has no air conditioning. The only way he can deal with the oppressive heat and boredom is to drink very cold wine, a lot of wine, especially Chardonnay and Rosé.

After taking a cold shower and slugging down more wine, Jake calls his father, Ron, on the phone. "Hey, Pop, how can you stand it here? Everything and everyone is orange! I believe I'm melting just like the witch in *The Wizard of Oz!*"

Ron interrupts his son and says, "Son, don't be so damn dramatic. Why don't you get out of the house and check out the town, and go connect with people?"

Jake knows this is a great idea and starts looking for the first bar.

As he walks through downtown, Jake sees a small sign that says, "Historic Walking Tour begins in 5 minutes." Jake thinks this would be a good way to learn the history and local folklore of the area. He walks up to the line and is greeted by the tour guide.

She smiles at Jake and says, "Hi, I'm Barbara Ann and I'm the docent for your tour. It will take approximately 45 minutes and ask me any questions along the way."

Being a history buff, an interest that was passed down by his mother, Jake took in all the information that she is sharing with the group.

When the tour is finished, Barbara Ann stares intently at Jake and says, "Looking at your nametag, Jake, how about joining me for a cup of coffee or a nice cold glass of Chardonnay?"

Jake replies, "Sure, why not. You lead the way since I'm new here. In fact, I just moved here yesterday."

Barbara Ann smiles and lets out a boisterous laugh and says, "Follow me, Jake. I know just the place."

CHAPTER 2

Broken

They sit in a small air-conditioned bar that has survived since the California Gold Rush. In the bar, there are many locals, or "townies," as Jake calls them. All the men wear plaid shirts with Wrangler jeans, cowboy boots, trucker baseball caps with their sunglasses resting on top, and have awfully long beards that make them look like extras from the *Duck Dynasty* television show. The women have on tight Daisy Duke denim shorts and halter tops that are two sizes too small, which accentuates their cleavage.

One of the townies, Clem, yells out to the group, "Hey, y'all, look at the Flatlander with the Polo shirt and shorts on!" They all glare at Jake, laugh, and return to their conversation. Of course, he is referring to Jake, with his clean cut and neat appearance.

Jake feels uncomfortable and out of place but smiles at Clem and goes back to his conversation with Barbara Ann.

Barbara Ann starts the conversation by saying, "Jake, I hope you liked the Historic Walking Tour. You know, I did all of the research, wrote it and taught all of the docents."

Jake knows this is a lie because his mother, Margaret, was the creator of this tour and was featured in the local newspaper for her accomplishment. Jake then wonders what other lies or half-truths he will listen to next from Barbara Ann.

Most of their conversation is friendly banter and small talk. Then suddenly Barbara Ann says, "Jake, I'm looking for a good man and you seem like a nice guy."

This amuses Jake and he interrupts her. "Barbara Ann, are you asking me out?"

She replies without hesitation, "Why, yes, I am. Whaddya say?"

Jake gives her his famous half-grin and says softly in order to not offend her, "Yes, I'm single, but seriously, I'm not looking right now. I just got out of a terrible marriage. In fact, the only things I got out of the divorce are my Mercedes, some clothes, and my cat, Josie. Barbara Ann, I need some time, but I very much appreciate the offer."

Hearing this news, Barbara Ann stands up, intentionally bumps the small table with her hip. This causes her glass of wine to spill right into Jake's lap, which makes him leap out of his chair. Barbara Ann starts to beeline towards the entrance of the bar, stops, turns around and looks intently at Jake. She then speaks in a voice that all the patrons can hear. "Fine. You'll see what it's like to find someone in this Godforsaken place. I, I, I hope you'll be as lonely as I am. Also, you can pay for my drink."

Jake interjects, "Barbara Ann, I apologize if I hurt your feelings. I'm just not ready to begin a relationship."

This makes Barbara Ann angry. She storms out and says, "Just wait and see, Jake. I'm the only woman in this town that's perfect for you."

Jake looks at the server and says, "Ick! I hope all of the women in this town aren't as volatile."

The server smiles at Jake while he pays the bill and Jake goes on his way, scratching his head and thinking to himself, *Shit, what have I done and why am I living here?*

Jake slowly walks back to his new home, and it is still blistering hot. He reaches into the refrigerator and grabs a bottle of expensive Chardonnay. He then opens the freezer and puts his head inside so he can feel the coolness of the air take over his sweaty body. He steps away and pours himself a tumbler of wine. He thinks to himself, *Hopefully the alcohol will numb this oppressive heat. It's unbearable!* The alcohol makes him sleepy, and just as he is about to fall asleep, his mobile phone rings, which startles him.

CHAPTER 3

Kinks Shirt

Jake answers the phone and it is his dad, Ron, who says, "Hey, Jake, how about you come with Mom and me to a wine party tonight? Our friend Rick's wife isn't feeling well. She can't go, so why don't you join us? You can be Rick's date, ha-ha!"

Jake thinks about this for a minute and says, "Sure, Pop, why not. What time? Let Rick know I'm not easy!"

Both men laugh and Ron agrees to pick up Jake at 6:00 P.M. to go to the party.

A few minutes before 6:00 P.M., Jake walks outside and down the driveway of his home and waits for Ron and his mother, Margaret, to pick him up. The heat has subsided as nighttime approaches. While Jake is waiting, he realizes he didn't check his mail. He pulls down the mailbox door and sees a note inside. He reaches for it and starts to read it. It says, "Jake, I'm sorry the way I acted today. Can we try again?" – Barbara Ann (209) 555-5555. Please, call me!" Jake thinks this gesture is kinda creepy. He then thinks to himself,

Ew, I wonder how she knows where I live? Did she follow me home? I can't wait to tell Mom and Dad about this strange day and the weird woman I met.

Soon, Ron, Margaret and Rick drive up and meet Jake. He climbs into the back seat of the car and starts sharing with them about his day, the strange lady he met at the Historical Walking Tour, and the note in his mailbox. Margaret asks Jake if he knew the docent's name that gave him the tour.

Jake tells her, "Barbara Ann."

This makes Margaret's blood boil and she exclaims, "That, that bitch! I suppose she took credit for all of it?"

Jake says, "Why, yes, she did, Mom. Why?"

Margaret shouts, "Because I did all of the research, wrote the script, trained the docents and reached out to the local media. When all the reporters came out here to do a story about the tour, Dad and I had to drive to San Francisco for my chemotherapy treatment. Of course, Barbara Ann met the reporters and told them this was her baby and she spent years working on it."

Jake then looks at his mom and says, "So, Mom, you didn't get the credit you deserve, and Barbara Ann got it all?"

Margaret shakes her head affirmatively. Jake knew this historical tour was very important to his mother and her legacy. Somehow, he had to find a way to preserve it for her.

When they pull up to the entrance to the winery, Jake jumps out of the car, lifts the trunk and grabs Margaret's wheelchair. He assembles it, helps his mother out of the car and wheels her to the front entrance. They wait for Ron and Rick. When they check in at the event, a beautiful young woman with a captivating smile and stunning hazel eyes greets them. Jake cannot take his eyes off her.

The hostess asks Jake for his name and he can only stammer, "JJJJJake."

The young woman smiles, cocks her head to the left, and speaks slowly towards him. "Well, Jake, you're not on the list, but I think I can squeeze you in."

Jake looks at her nametag, which spells "Kate" and says, "Thank you, Kate. I appreciate it. By the way, I'm not trying to come on to you, but you have the most amazing eyes I have ever seen."

Kate smiles coyly and says, "Thank you, Jake, it must be the blouse I'm wearing. It accentuates my eyes."

Jake then nervously replies, "Yes, yes, that must be it. Besides, the Kinks are one of my favorite bands."

After this brief exchange, Jake wheels Margaret to the table where they will be sitting. Everyone at the table is a friend of Ron and Margaret. They begin to tease Jake about his exchange with Kate.

Jake tells them, "I've never been that captivated or nervous around a woman. She caught me off guard. I also didn't see a ring on her finger." This prompts a big "Yahoo!" from Jake.

Everybody at the table laughs heartily.

Just then, Margaret's best friend, Rusty, approaches their table and says, "Hey all, what's so funny?"

Margaret replies, "Jake is quite smitten with Kate, you know, the pretty young woman that checked us all in."

Rusty says excitedly, "Really? I've known Kate and her family since she was a little girl." Just then, Rusty looks back at the group and says jokingly, "I've always wanted to be a matchmaker!" She then turns to Jake and says, "Jake, let me provide you with a proper introduction."

Jake says, "Sure, Rusty, lead the way."

Rusty and Jake walk up to Kate, who is now serving wine to other guests at a bar away from the dining tables.

Rusty says, "Kate, I'd like to introduce you to Jake. His mom is my best friend. Jake, I'd like for you to meet Kate. I've known her and her family since she was a little girl. Kate is the pride of our community. Straight-A student, attended the best colleges, lived and worked abroad, and we never thought she would either look or come back."

Everybody smiles, then Jake speaks up and says, "Kate, do you live here now?"

Kate replies, "No, I live in San Francisco. I'm just helping my friends out tonight. They own the winery."

Jake smiles and says, "Ah, San Francisco, my favorite city in the whole world. You are incredibly lucky to live there. In fact, I just moved from there to live here, to help take care of my mom."

Jake then proceeds to order wine for the table of his parents' friends. The activity of Jake going up to get more wine for the table becomes a continuous habit throughout the evening. It also gives him a good excuse to exchange a few flirtatious comments with Kate. Finally, Jake musters up the courage to ask Kate for her phone number and business card.

Kate thinks for a few seconds and says, "Sure, if you wait here for a few minutes, I'll go up to the house and get one out of my purse."

Jake waits for her to return, which seems like an eternity. All his parents' friends start to leave the party. Just then, Ron, Margaret and Rick ask him what he's doing standing around looking lost.

Jake says to them, "I'm waiting for Kate to return with her business card."

Rick laughs and says, "Do you think she's ditchin' ya?"

Jake replies, "I don't think so. She seems genuinely nice and interested."

As he says this, Kate approaches the group and hands her card to Jake and says, "I'm sorry it took so long, Jake. I had to dig down to the bottom of my handbag to find one."

Margaret then says to Kate, "So, Kate, we hope you like that Jake was our server tonight. We all thought this would give you two a chance to talk and get to know each other a bit."

Kate then speaks to the group. "Yes, I thought it was very cute and sweet how he doted over his mother, but honestly at first, I thought he had a huge drinking problem!"

Everybody laughed and Jake promised Kate he would call her soon.

Once they were in the car. Margaret says to Jake, "I really like Kate. I have a really good feeling about her."

Jake responds, "Yes, Mom, so do I. So do I."

CHAPTER 4

Perfect

Over the course of the next several weeks, Jake and Kate talk for hours on the phone. They really get to know each other and become fast friends. Jake then asks Kate out for a date. There is an upcoming "Ragin' Cajun Party" at a local historic hotel. At the party, a famous Zydeco band will perform while everyone dances, authentic Cajun cuisine will be served, and the whole evening will be a blast. Jake thinks this will be something memorable and different for their first date. However, there is a big problem. The event is sold out. This does not deter Jake. He's a resourceful and creative person and asks the event coordinator if he can volunteer to help set up for the party. Hopefully, this will garner him two tickets to the event. The coordinator agrees and Jake's first task is to climb up a 50-foot ladder and string lights across the tall and majestic oak trees. After several unsuccessful attempts of trying to lasso the lights over the tree branches, Jake falls onto the mushy green lawn and into a huge pile of goose poop! "Yuck!" he exclaims all the while telling himself that a date with Kate is worth this crappy effort.

Kate agrees to the special occasion date and appreciates all the effort Jake put into it. On the day of the date, she drives her convertible BMW to Jake's house and gently pulls into the driveway. The first thing they do when they see each other is embrace tightly and kiss slowly and passionately. Josie, Jake's cat, is not very happy about this stranger coming into their home. In fact, she is very jealous. The only human she loves and trusts is Jake. He rescued her from a horrible situation where her previous owners locked her in a garage with several Dobermans. She was traumatized, and it took months for Josie to trust anyone, but she finally warmed up to Jake and never left his side. Jake always jokes with his friends that Josie is his second wife, because she will meow loudly if he is late coming home or doesn't follow his normal routine. Josie seems to be okay with Kate and walks back into the house. Kate asks if she can freshen up before they leave for the party. Jake points her into the direction of the guest bathroom and pours them each a glass of Rosé with delicately placed freshly picked blackberries in crystal wineglasses.

Suddenly, a loud scream comes from the guest bathroom. It's Kate, she yells out the door, "Uh, Jake, your cat just pooped in the bathroom sink."

Jake replies to her, "Oh, dear. She must be jealous of you, Kate. Let me clean this up. Go ahead and use my bathroom."

Jake drives his car down the windy and dark road to where the party is taking place. It is an old historic and haunted hotel that dates to the Gold Rush. It is the perfect setting for a Cajun party. Christmas lights hang in the trees as well as the roofline of the front porch deck, Zydeco music is playing loudly, and the aroma of boiling shrimp and jambalaya permeates the air. Jake and Kate sit at a table with Rusty and her husband, Robert. They all dance, sing and eat amazing authentic Cajun cuisine. It is a long evening and first date, but Kate and Jake are full of infatuation and admiration for each other. They leave the party and go back to Jake's house. Of course, Josie greets them at the door by meowing loudly because it is so late. They both laugh and reach down to pet the cat. Josie surprises Jake when she lets Kate pet and pick her up.

Jake then says, "She never lets anyone do that. She must trust and like you. That's a very good sign."

Jake then reaches for Kate and gives her a long and languishing kiss. He hands her a glass of wine, and they gracefully glide into Jake's bedroom.

CHAPTER 5

Werewolves of London

Early the next morning, there is a loud knock on the front door. Jake springs out of bed like a piece of toast, with Josie following to see who this could be at such an early hour. Jake opens the door, sees the orange sky and Barbara Ann's hair that matches the hue of the background sky. Jake keeps the door partially closed until Barbara Ann tries pushing her way into the house holding a bowl of apples and says, "Aren't you going to invite me in? I thought you might be hungry, so I brought you these beautiful, fresh-picked apples."

As Barbara Ann makes her way into the house, Josie growls and hisses loudly. Barbara Ann then picks up an apple and just as she is going to throw it at the cat, Kate walks into the room, wearing Jake's bathrobe, and yells at Barbara Ann, "STOP it! Are you crazy? I don't know who you think you are but leave right now!"

Barbara Ann walks out in a huff, looks at Jake and says, "You'll be sorry, Jake!" She then turns to Kate, turns up her nose and says under her breath, "I saw him first and he's mine!" and walks out the front door. As she heads out to her car, she pulls out her car keys from her purse and deliberately digs them deeply into the side panel of Kate's brand-new BMW.

Jake, Kate and Josie walk back inside and make coffee, tea and a bowl of milk for Josie. Josie even sits on Kate's lap. Jake whips up a simple continental breakfast and starts to reach for the apples.

Kate then says, "I'm not so sure about eating those."

Jake says to her, "Why?"

Kate responds, "Well, there are rumors in this community that Barbara Ann killed her husband by poisoning him with apples."

Jake replies, "Such a waste of good fruit, but in the trash they go." Jake then feverishly and deliberately scrubs his hands with the strongest soap he can find.

Jake and Kate spend the morning and early afternoon sitting out on Jake's patio talking, kissing, and getting to know each other. Time goes by quickly and Kate needs to leave soon to drive back to San Francisco. When it is time for them to say goodbye, they walk out towards Kate's car and see the deep indentation across the side of her car.

Kate is furious and can only think of who did this. She then tells Jake, "I'll file a police report when I get home, and please stay away from that woman. She's bat-shit crazy!"

Jake shakes his head in agreement, kisses Kate goodbye, waves as she leaves, and walks back into his house. Once inside, he sees the red light of his home answering machine flickering. Jake did not hear the phone ring, so he presses the play button. The voice on the message was oh so eerily familiar. It is Barbara Ann. Her voice is angry. "I told you, you'll be sorry, Jake. I don't know who that girl is you are with, but both of you will be very, very sorry! I mean it. Besides, I have a new boyfriend and his name is Andy, and he can kick your ass. Doesn't this make you jealous and afraid, Jake?"

Jake knows this is all too weird and Kate is right. He needs to stay far away from Barbara Ann.

The following week, Kate calls Jake and says, "I have a surprise date for you. I don't know if it's going to top yours, but I believe we'll have fun. Come on down to the city and I'll show you a little about me."

Jake replies, "Wow, Kate, I'm really intrigued. Tell me when, where and what should I wear?"

Kate laughs and says, "Meet me on Saturday at 10:00 A.M. at this address in Sacramento." She then hangs up.

Jake immediately put the information in his calendar and Googled the address. "Wow!" Jake exclaims. "This is the address for the FBI Field Office in Sacramento. I wonder how this is going to be a date?"

On Saturday, Jake walks out his front door, picks up a small bag of apples placed there by Barbara Ann, and tosses them into the trash. He then gets into his silver Mercedes Benz E350 Sedan with the sky roof open to meet Kate. He wants to be as cool as possible and have his salt-and-pepper curly locks look as windblown as possible. Jake pulls into the driveway of the FBI Field Office, parks the car, checks his teeth and hair in the review mirror, and heads towards the front door.

CHAPTER 6

When a Man Loves a Woman

To his surprise, Jake's name is on the entrance list and, after showing his I.D. and getting a visitor's badge, he is free to walk into a waiting room. Just as he is about to sit down, he hears a familiar voice that says, "Hi, Jake! I wasn't sure you would make it."

Jake smiles when he recognizes Kate's voice and says to her, "I wouldn't miss this chance for the world."

Kate escorts Jake to a nearby shooting range, where many agents practice their skills. Suddenly the agents see Kate, drop their guns and yell simultaneously, "Kate, are you coming back? We miss you!"

One agent says, "Hey all, Kill Shot Kate is here!"

Then another agent pipes in, "Whaddya mean? She's back?"

After this exchange, Jake asks Kate, "So what does this mean?"

Kate tells Jake, "If you really want to know. I'll fill you in later. Let's go have some fun."

Just then one of the agents interrupts them and tells Jake,

"Did you know Kill Shot, here, graduated first in her class at Quantico, and retired as the most respected criminal profiler in the FBI's Behavioral Analysis Unit?"

Kate expects Jake to run and head for the door as have all of the other men she has dated. Jake smiles at her, and just as he's about to speak, one of the other agents walks up to him and says, "Do I know you? You look so familiar. Have we worked together?"

Jake recognizes him but says, "I, uh, don't remember."

Kate smiles, then motions to Jake to follow her to the shooting range. An agent hands them loaded pistols, eye guards, and earmuffs. Kate signals to Jake to go first.

Reluctantly, he fires the pistol at the target and misses terribly. He mouths to Kate, "I'm rusty!"

Immediately, Kate empties all the bullets in the magazine of her pistol, all "kill" shots.

Jake looks at Kate's target, thinks to himself, *How embarrassing and impressive at the same time.* Jake then motions to Kate to lift up her earmuffs. She does and he says to her humbly, "I'm just warming up."

They both shoot at the targets for a long time. Jake is getting better with each round and Kate mouths, "Not bad, rookie." However, he cannot compete with Kate's expert marksmanship skills. Both are starting to tire out and Kate says, "I know a great lunch place nearby. Are you hungry?"

Jake replies, "Affirmative, Special Agent."

Kate looks at him, smiles and says, "Let's go eat. I know just the place."

They walk to a café that is across the street. As they cross, a green AMC Gremlin pulls out in front of them and nearly hits both of them. Jake grabs Kate in a protective manner, yells at the driver, chases the car, and throws the target practice papers at it.

Kate looks at Jake and says, "Dude, calm down. The driver probably didn't see us."

Jake then says, "I know, I know, but you almost got hit, Kate. My biggest pet peeve is rude, very rude and inconsiderate people."

Kate looks at him admiringly and appreciates his chivalry.

When they walk into the café, the entire staff recognizes Kate. The hostess says to her, "The usual table?"

Kate nods in agreement and they are escorted to a table towards the back of the restaurant. Kate instinctually sits facing the door and tells Jake old habits are hard to break.

"Do you mind if I sit here?"

Jake nods affirmatively and says, "As long as a bullet doesn't hit me in the back of the head."

Kate then looks quizzically at Jake and says, "Only someone with law enforcement training would make that comment. Also, why did that agent at the shooting range swear he knows you? What's up with that?"

Jake then speaks slowly and deliberately and tells Kate, "I always wanted to work in law enforcement, especially the FBI, but I became an art insurance investigator, because I needed the money to raise my first family. As you know, the FBI doesn't pay well for new agents. However, I did receive a lot of training when I was in the FBI academy. After I dropped out, many of the trainers were upset with me because they all felt I had the right temperament and would make an excellent agent. And the gentleman at the shooting range, well, he and I worked together a few times on the FBI Art Crime Team. In fact, we spent a lot of time investigating the Isabella Gardner museum art heist in 1990. I'm sorry, Kate, I didn't fess up. Now, you know my back story. I hope you won't think differently of me?"

Abruptly, Kate stands up, extends her arms towards Jake across the table and says, "Jake, I love you even more! By the way, do you know who stole the art at the museum?"

Jake smiles and says to her quietly, "If I tell you, then I'll have to kill you!"

Both of them laugh heartily. After this moment, Jake knew he was going to marry Kate and raise a family together. One year later, they did.

CHAPTER 7

Moth to a Flame

Easter was here and it was one of Margaret's favorite holidays. She loves to watch the children scream with delight while running for candy and eggs at a local winery. This was a bucolic setting for an amazing Easter Brunch. Ron, Margaret, Kate, and Jake are sitting at a beautiful outside table. Jake makes sure there is plenty of room for Margaret's wheelchair.

Just as they are toasting each other with Mimosas, Barbara Ann approaches them, sneers at Kate and proceeds to pour a Mimosa on Kate's lap. She yells at Margaret, "I always hated you, Mrs. Smarty Pants! The Historical Walking Tour was my idea."

This ruckus causes Jake to jump up, try to catch as much of the spilt liquid, yells at Barbara Ann to leave now and to stay away from him, his family and especially his wife, Kate. Jake then starts to charge at Barbara Ann, but winery security officers arrive on the scene and escort Barbara Ann out quickly and forcibly. Just as this happens, an apple falls from Barbara Ann's purse and rolls into the next room.

Margaret says, "Jake, she's not worth it. She's fuckin' nuts and if you keep this up, something terrible is going to happen to both you and Kate!"

Jake agrees with his mother, exhales, and sits back down at the table.

The rest of the meal is enjoyable, and they all have a good time.

As Kate leaves the table for the restroom, Margaret leans over to Jake and says, "Jake, you finally got it right. I really like Kate. She's perfect for you and a great fit for our family. Hang on to this one. She's a real keeper!"

Jake and Ron smile in agreement.

Jake winks at his mother and says, "Mom, I promise. If we have a girl, we'll name her in honor of you!"

Chapter 8

Fix You

As the months go by, Margaret is getting weaker as the cancer overtakes her frail body. She is skin and bones and decides to stop chemotherapy. Her comfort is God, the church community, and having her family by her side. One day, she asks Jake to call his siblings to come home to say goodbye. A few days later, September 11th, Margaret passes away at home peacefully with the family by her side.

The memorial service is overflowing with guests in the quaint and historic local church. The sunlight breaks through the stained-glass windows, and a rainbow ends on top of Margaret's casket. The church choir sings many of her favorite songs and her children, grandchildren and many friends share stories about a beloved wife, mother, and friend. The wake is attended by the entire community and lasts well into the night.

After his mother's passing, Jake believes he and Kate will leave this small town and move back to the big city, where he feels he belongs. He frequently shares with his dad that he feels like a "fish out of water" in this small mountain town. The night after Margaret's funeral, Jake has the most vivid and memorable dream of his life. When Jake awoke, he picks up his cellphone and immediately calls his father. He asks him to come over to the house.

Kate is enjoying her morning coffee at the kitchen table, when she looks up and can see by the expression on Jake's face that something on his mind is urgent.

Jake then says very quickly, "Hey, Pop, you and Kate aren't going to believe the dream I had last night. I saw Mom, wearing her favorite blue and white polo shirt, doing cartwheels. She told me, which was more like pure thought than a conversation, 'Tell everyone I'm free and it's beautiful here, and thank you so much for taking care of Dad and looking after him. But sweetheart, please watch Dad's drinking and yours too. It's not good for you.'"

Suddenly, Ron begins to weep silently, then explosively. This makes Kate cry too.

After composing herself, Kate says, "Jake, we can't move from here. Last night, you made a covenant with your mother to look after your dad."

Jake nods his head and says, "Yes, Kate, I did and I won't let her down."

CHAPTER 9

Barbara Ann

Barbara Ann frequently hosts her teacher colleagues at her home for dinner or for a book club meeting. Yet this activity ends soon, because dinner always consists of crackers with a small portion of canned tuna on top, or stale bread and salami. This "meal" is always served with spoiled cheap wine and apples to follow for dessert.

Her guests cannot bear the eye-watering aroma of ammonia and pungent odor of animal feces. What also becomes a concern is how demanding and even cruel she is to her own children regarding punishment for simple "kid stuff." This alarms her fellow teachers, and they do not accept any more of Barbara Ann's shenanigans and invitations. This upsets her. In her mind, nobody likes or respects her.

This always stirs up bad memories in Barbara Ann of the rejection by Jeff, her husband of many years. He fell out of love with her, because she was demanding, bossy, a bully and would frequently tell him he was a loser and a wuss. He could not take any more of Barbara Ann's increasingly eccentric behavior of hoarding and stacking newspapers and magazines on the floor of their home. It was a disgusting trail allowing one to move from one room to the other. Jeff demanded that Barbara Ann seek help, but she refused and always told him he was the crazy one! When Jeff moved out, he left so quickly that he didn't take his prized gun collection, which remains in the basement of the modest home. Because Jeff left so abruptly and disappeared from view, the townies spread rumors Barbara Ann killed him by poisoning him with tainted apples. They accused her of being a witch. All the couple friends they share abandoned Barbara Ann. When she thinks of it, it angers her and makes her feel rejected by her peers and the community—again.

However, Barbara Ann knows deep in her heart that something is going to change this dreary life. She makes the decision to run for the local school board. Suddenly, the alarm clock wakes her up to the sounds of the Beach Boys familiar tune *"Barbara Ann."* It is Election Day, and she feels incredibly happy. She knows deep down in her psyche she is going to win her campaign to be a school board trustee. Gone will be all of the public humiliation, teasing, and taunting by the townies that call her "Batty Barbara Ann" to her face, while laughing at her. She will be vindicated, because she believes she, and she alone, can fire the school superintendent that terminated her employment as a tenured elementary school teacher. Asphyxiating frogs and teaching a kindergarten class what death is like was the last straw for the superintendent. He fired Barbara Ann immediately. Even the powerful teachers union didn't resist the dismissal.

Barbara Ann is volunteering to be a poll worker today, and she puts on her good-luck outfit that consists of a flowing and torn oversized t-shirt (that matches her hair color), well-worn black pedal pushers and splattered paint-designed sandals. She knows she is looking good. Before she walks out her front door, she looks in a wall mirror, puts on her favorite red beret, turns it ever so slightly to the right and says to herself, "I'm an elected official, and I'm ready for a fight!"

She starts up her old green AMC Gremlin that is full of dents, because she has been in several hit-and-run accidents that are always her fault. Since she does not want to have the DMV revoke her driver's license, she always pays the fines. Money is not an issue for Barbara Ann. Her father invested well in successful corporations, and this inheritance provides her with a steady source of income in addition to her teacher's retirement.

When Barbara Ann pulls into the parking lot of the polling place, she rolls down the driver's-side window and greets all the lined-up voters with her infamous bellicose laugh. This makes all of those in line cringe, put their fingers in their ears and mumble to themselves, "That Fuckin' Batty Barbara Ann."

CHAPTER 10

Eye of the Tiger

Barbara Ann's competitor in this campaign is Jake. Many community members begged him to run against Barbara Ann, because revenge was her only purpose and passion for being elected. Also, Jake served on a prior school board for a big city and was going to use this experience to help guide the schools in his community. He had thoughts of running for higher office later, so this could be a good starting place. Jake's view of the world is that a person is either right or wrong, innocent or guilty. He also despises bullies! He is the youngest of four children and constantly had to fight his way to gain attention or even get enough food. He was a chubby kid and picked on by his siblings and schoolmates. Jake is always the protector of the underdog, which has gotten him into fights in childhood and his career. Jake has a "hair-trigger" temper and goes into a rage when he encounters injustice, bullying or people just being rude.

In fact, one day, he was in line at the local grocery store when a customer in front of him was screaming at the cashier for no reason. This went on for a few minutes, but it seemed like an eternity to Jake. He went to the defense of the sobbing cashier and yelled at the bully to leave her alone. The man called Jake an asshole and told him to butt out. This was the wrong thing to do. Jake's face turned bright red, and his anger boiled over. He charged the man and told him sternly to leave or his face would be unrecognizable. The man looked at the cashier and then at Jake, and scurried quickly out of the store. The incident made other customers in the grocery store clap and cheer. Jake did not hear any of this, but stepped around the counter and asked the woman if she was ok. Still shaking and trying to catch her breath, she thanked Jake, "You're my hero!" Jake smiled, relished the attention, paid for his groceries, and knew he did the right thing.

On Election Day, the precinct captain assigns Barbara Ann to monitor the Provisional Ballots from voters that forgot or are late mailing in their absentee ballots. By dropping off their ballot and handing it to a poll worker, their vote counts – a common practice in many rural communities. For most of the day, Barbara Ann sits on a stool and sings Broadway show tunes at the top of her lungs, which is a big distraction to the voters and precinct workers. Very few provisional ballots make their way to her. But as the day goes on, she starts to become nervous, because many voters hand their ballots to her to make sure it counts for their friend and the most qualified candidate, Jake. Barbara Ann promptly and ever so deviously tears the ballots up and throws them in the trash.

That night, Jake has a small election night party at a popular local restaurant with his family, supporters, and campaign volunteers. The room is filled with excitement, laughter, music, and a lot of champagne toasts. The early returns show Jake has a narrow lead over Barbara Ann. As the evening goes on, Jake's lead dwindles and Barbara Ann's vote count inches ahead by 35 votes! It is now midnight and Jake's victory party is a bust. When he finally goes to bed, he is losing by 58 votes. Jake is exhausted from the long campaign, coffee klatches, service club speeches and doesn't understand why he is losing to Batty Barbara Ann.

The next morning, Jake wakes up and walks out the front door of his home and down the long driveway to retrieve the local newspaper to review the final election results. When he unfolds the curled and slightly torn newspaper, he is extremely angry, because on the front cover and lead story is a picture of Barbara Ann with a caption that reads: "Precinct Volunteer, Barbara Ann, assists a voter on Election Day." This makes Jake fume with anger. County and state law mandates that all candidates must be 100 feet from a polling place. Jake is perplexed as he thinks to himself, *How can a candidate work as a poll volunteer?* He then runs into his house, shows the newspaper to Kate, who is furious. Kate responds immediately by calling the County Registrar's office and is told, "Gee, this has never happened before, and maybe in the future we should change things so this type of thing won't happen again." After this ignorant response, Kate's temper flares, so she calls the County District Attorney's office to report this blatant abuse of the election process. She is placed on hold and eventually hung up on. "Goddamn Banana Republic!" exclaims Kate. She then sits down and rifles off an email to the D.A. No reply would ever be received.

Jake starts receiving phone calls from members of the community in disbelief that he lost to Barbara Ann. One astute friend said, "It must've been because she used 'Retired

Teacher' as her occupation on the ballot. This way, folks that don't know either one of you would probably choose her." Jake believes this makes sense and goes to his laptop to see the most updated returns. However, one newspaper catches him by surprise, because the reporter labels him as a "City Slicker and Flatlander," both derogatory terms locals use to describe folks that were not born in this county. Jake knew this characterization did not help him win an election in his new hometown.

CHAPTER 11

How Long (Has This Been Going On)

There were no hanging chads, but the election is a real cliffhanger. Barbara Ann's vote count is decreasing by the minute as more provisional and absentee ballots come in. First it was 58, then 49, then 45, to 40. This went on for the entire month of November. December slips in, and Barbara Ann's lead falls to just 35 votes. The election results must be certified by December 7th, so the count continues day and night. On December 7th, the final total is announced: Barbara Ann – 15,898; Jake – 15,863. Barbara Ann is declared the winner by 35 votes.

Jake's mobile phone is vibrating so much it falls off the armchair. Many good friends and colleagues call to express their condolences and want to know if he is going to demand a recount of the vote. Jake thinks about this, asks Kate for her advice, and begins researching how this process works. He Googles: "How much does a recount cost?" He learns the process is free if he wins, but if he loses it costs $250.00 for every vote.

Jake does the math in his head and thinks to himself, *If I have 15,863 votes now and if that slightly increases, and I still don't win, this would cost Kate and I over $8,000 dollars! Although I'm the better candidate, it's not worth spending this amount of money on an election.*

Giving up is not a part of Jake's DNA; however, the election result is certified and Batty Barbara Ann wins. She, not Jake, is going to lead and guide the vision of the school district. Jake shakes his head at this thought, because his child is going to attend their local elementary school within this jurisdiction. He often wonders if his child and others will be okay with Barbara Ann as the "Gatekeeper" of this school district for four years. The next day, Jake posts on Facebook a picture of his infant son in a onesie that says: "It's all good!" The image goes viral and makes the cover of the local online newspaper.

After the certification of the election, Barbara Ann steps into high gear, because she is going to be a hero and fire the Superintendent of Public Schools that wronged her. She barges into the school district's administrative office briskly and forces her way through security and staff members into Dr. Matthews' office. The joke is on Barbara Ann, because Dr. Matthews immediately resigned from his position after the vote was ratified. He packed up his belongings, said goodbye and good luck to his handpicked staff members, and briskly left the building never to be seen or heard from again. This infuriates Barbara Ann, because she will not get her payback or her revenge. After all, this is the reason she ran for the school board!

The next day, the Board of Trustees is meeting to search for a new superintendent. Barbara Ann bursts into the small conference room one hour late, always her modus operandi.

She greets everybody in the room with her familiar bellicose laugh, but is dismissed and ignored. She then reaches into a small brown paper bag and grabs some apples and offers them to her fellow trustees. All of them look at each other, turn to Barbara Ann and politely refuse her offer of potentially poison apples.

CHAPTER 12

Respect

Barbara Ann is seething, because she is not granted the respect and dignity she believes she deserves by being an elected official. She feels she is an equal, because she is now "part of the club" and one of the Board of Trustees. Walter, the school board president, immediately takes charge of the meeting and begins to narrow down the search of possible superintendent candidates. With school reconvening soon after the Christmas break, the district needs a new and effective leader. The board votes 4 to 1 with one "Nay." That of course is Barbara Ann. She does not like this new administrator, because he has he has extremely limited experience and is currently the director of an online educational institution.

Barbara Ann yells, "How can this person lead this district without working with children in the classroom or, or, or let alone see any students? He's a bad, awfully bad choice." All the other school board members ignore her and move on with the agenda and vote in favor of the new superintendent.

Barbara Ann feels the others are ignoring and dismissing her, which really pisses her off.

Barbara Ann knows, deep in her psyche, from this day on, that she will save the school district as a lone wolf and gain the respect of the entire community. She feels she is invincible and does not need her doctor prescribed medication for what she addresses as "the blues." She believes it makes her feel and look puffy. Barbara Ann also has become self-conscious of the extra pounds she has put on because of the anti-depressants, after she and Andy broke up.

Over the weeks as the positive effects of the medication wear off, Barbara Ann goes on a rampage. She starts by walking unannounced into a first-grade class and chastising the teacher, in front of her students, by telling her she does not know how to teach. Barbara Ann then begins teaching a lesson. She is once again compelled to demonstrate to five-year-olds what death is like and proceeds to choke a frog that she carries in her coat pocket.

Barbara Ann proclaims, "Now kiddos, you see the frog is free because it's dead. Isn't this beautiful and peaceful?" The children gasp and cry. Two students vomit. The children screech, "How can she do that to our town's mascot—Freddy the Frog?"

Aww, the fun is just beginning, thinks Barbara Ann. She barges into the next classroom and proceeds to throw paint at the students' art projects, rips work off several walls, calls one of the teachers a bitch and the school principal, Kurt, a wuss.

Barbara Ann in a state of exaltation starts to stalk her next victim—a colleague that ended their friendship many years before because of Barbara Ann's increasingly strange behavior.

No one dares reject Barbara Ann. When she is ready to pounce on her prey, she is grabbed on the arm by Kurt, who escorts her out of the classroom. Barbara Ann resists, takes a swing at him and proceeds to march into the girls' restroom. Loud bursts of shouting expletives are exchanged through the closed bathroom door.

Kurt yells into his walkie-talkie to the school secretary to call the county sheriff's office, because this is the only way to end this standoff. Fortunately, there are no children in the restroom, because Barbara Ann uses the toilet, stands up from the toilet seat, reaches for drapes at a nearby window, yanks them down, and proceeds to clean up after herself. When she finishes, she smears feces on the toilet, bathroom stalls, walls, doors, and writes **"WUSS"** in bold and dark brown letters on the mirror above the bathroom sink.

Several female staff members burst into the bathroom and do their best to try and calm her down and lead her off the campus. She resists and tells one of the teachers, Miss Waugh, to take her hands off her because she is violating her space and molesting her. Miss Waugh releases her grip as she sees not one, but three county sheriff cars pull into the school parking lot. Unfortunately, for the officers, the school dismissal bell sounds and children begin running out of their classrooms. Several anxious parents drive into the parking lot not expecting to see the spectacle taking place in front of them.

One of the officers runs to where Barbara Ann is standing and grabs her. She resists and tosses him aside like a paper doll. The second uniformed man tries to no avail. Not having medication in her system while being in a manic state, Barbara Ann is exhibiting the strength of the Incredible Hulk. Finally, the third officer runs to Barbara Ann from behind and places a chokehold on her. This seems to subdue her, but it just agitates her more because he has "poked the belly of the beast!" It takes all three officers to wrestle Barbara Ann to the ground and "hogtie" her. Meanwhile, she keeps screaming at the top of her lungs, "You can't do this to me. I'm Barbara Ann and I'm an elected official. I'm going to have you all fired! Also, if you didn't already know, Kurt is a wuss and Miss Waugh is a bitch, and, and, and stop molesting me, you mother fuckers!"

Finally, an officer squeezes Barbara Ann into the back seat of one of the sheriff's vehicles and she is driven off to the county jail. As this occurs an apple rolls down the pavement and is squashed by the patrol car leaving the school.

CHAPTER 13

Crazy

This is not a good day at Jack London Elementary School. Many of the parents huddle together and discuss amongst themselves what they can do to remove Barbara Ann from the school board and keep her away from their children.

The PTA President, Sharon, takes command and says to the group, "What if we start a recall against her? It will take all of us to gather enough signatures to remove her from office."

Everyone believes this is the best idea. Immediately, they begin plotting their campaign against Barbara Ann. Meanwhile, Kurt files the first of many restraining orders against Barbara Ann to keep her off the campus and as far away from him as possible.

The next day, Barbara Ann is placed on her first of many 51/50 psychiatric holds. She is booked at the county jail for misdemeanor assault and then whisked off to a mental health facility several hundred miles away. The doctors on staff believe Barbara Ann is a dangerous threat and will do harm to herself.

They keep her in the facility for several weeks. They monitor her progress and force her to take medications. Finally, she begins to stabilize, promises the doctors she will keep taking her meds, and is sent home.

However, there is a big problem. Barbara Ann has no money or credit cards with her. So how is she going to get home? She knows she must start calling people and lie by telling them she was staying in a hotel, and all her credit cards were stolen. Bizarrely, she calls Jake, Kurt, several current school board members, and all reject her plea for help. This angers Barbara Ann. No one disrespects her! She is so desperate she calls her ex-boyfriend, Andy. He will not rescue her but makes arrangements for a taxi company to pick her up, and she'll have to reimburse him for the cost. Barbara Ann agrees and returns home. Andy never did get his money back.

When Barbara Ann returns home, she walks into every business and demands free meals, free wine from the many tasting rooms that line Main Street, free haircuts, and free clothing because she is an important elected official. With her erratic behavior, almost every business in town has a restraining order against her except for the local historic hotel. One evening at the hotel bar, she orders a drink from Bob, the owner. He thinks Barbara Ann is just eccentric, but not crazy. He knows she suffers from mental illness and tries to be kind to her, because his mother suffers from the same plight.

Barbara Ann orders a double shot of Absinthe, knowing full well that alcohol and her medication don't mix. When she finishes her last sip of "The Green Fairy," her ex-boyfriend, Andy, who is very drunk, grabs her from behind. She does not flinch. He then reaches up around her waist, and she does not move a muscle. Andy then grabs her breasts and she freezes.

Andy laughs as do the other patrons. He then drives home and goes to bed. After experiencing the ridicule and public humiliation, Barbara Ann calls the County Sheriff's Department to report an assault that just took place. It takes the first officer over two hours to respond because there have been so many "bullshit" 911 calls from Barbara Ann, and the department assumes it is one more. The dispatcher takes the report and sends an officer to drive to Barbara Ann's home and interview her. When the discussion is complete, he gets in his patrol car and drives to Andy's home to get his version of the story. Andy is woken up by a loud banging on his front door.

The officer yells, "Andy, I know you're in there. Open up!"

As Andy opens the door, the smell of rancid whiskey permeates his breath.

The officer says affirmatively, "Andy, I believe you know why I'm here."

Without a beat, Andy stammers, "YYYeah, I grabbed her tttits. She used to be my girlfriend; you know."

The officer immediately handcuffs Andy, puts him in the back of his squad car and drives him to the county jail.

Because there are no forthcoming witnesses, and the hotel's video camera inside the bar is disabled, an assault charge will not apply, but the officer charges Andy with a DUI. Andy posts bail and his new girlfriend, Gloria, drives him home, kisses him on the forehead, and places him into bed.

The next day, the town is filled with excitement as many tourists are arriving for the annual Concourse d' Elegance. The street is lined with classic, exotic, and expensive automobiles. Many tourists go to the hotel bar to converse and swap stories about their passion of collecting classic cars. Andy is in the bar as Barbara Ann walks in.

She sees Andy and starts screaming at the top of her lungs, "You creep, you molester, I'm going to send you to jail right now!"

This scene shocks the bar patrons. The bartender yells at Barbara Ann to get out and calls for Bob to remove this crazy and disruptive person. Bob has no choice but to ask her to leave and never return again. Later that night when the guests retire for the evening, Barbara Ann pulls out of her purse a can of black spray paint. She proceeds to paint the windows of the hotel with the words **"Don't Patronize This Business, Anyone Who Goes Here Will be Raped and Molested**." Her tirade continues by ripping plants from the ground and throwing them at the hotel doors. She then removes holiday decorations, leaves old hotel menus on the cars in the hotel's visitor parking lot with the message **"Don't Eat, Drink or Stay Here. It's a Haven for Molesters!"** She then keys a beautifully restored 1958 Edsel that will most likely win first in its class at the Concourse d' Elegance. Thankfully for Bob, the hotel's outside video cameras recorded this frenetic scene.

Bob reviews the camera disc and has no choice but to file a police report for the vandalism that took place at his hotel. He was hoping the damages would exceed the threshold for a felony because this would remove Barbara Ann from office and hopefully restore peace in the community. Unfortunately, the amount fell short and Barbara Ann is charged and arrested with five misdemeanors. Thus began the first of over twenty misdemeanor charges filed against Barbara Ann over the following months.

During her tenure on the school board, Barbara Ann throws meeting agendas at school staff, members of the public, and her colleagues if they disagree with her position or vote. This makes many in the community afraid of her irrational and volatile temper tantrums. However, this behavior fuels the recall efforts to oust Barbara Ann. The next day, many community members stand outside supermarkets, banks, post offices, stores and tasting rooms to gather the necessary signatures for a recall. After many hours of trying to collect signatures, the canvassers are feeling discouraged, because the local citizens do not want to sign the petition for fear that Barbara Ann will retaliate and harm them.

Barbara Ann catches wind of this activity taking place and writes the first of her infamous manifestos. It is addressed to "Dear Recall Committee Captain." The letter goes on to state what a wonderful mother, wife, church member and especially effective elected official she is. Then there are ten pages of gibberish, nonsense, and a hitlist of people that should be fired at the school district. After this episode, the recall is called off, because there are not enough signatures. Many community members fear for their safety.

Barbara Ann tastes victory once again because of the failed recall effort and is off her psychiatric prescribed medications. She walks into downtown and starts kissing men, women, children, dogs, cats and even neighbors who despise her. Throughout the years, her neighbors' car was keyed on many occasions, windows broken, and plants killed because they would not pay attention or speak to her. When she returns home, Barbara Ann bursts into her neighbors', Burt and Cathy's house to tell them the good news about the recall. Burt proceeds to tell her that he was the first one to sign the petition and to leave his house immediately. Burt escorts her out the door, and Barbara Ann yells at him to stop molesting her, reaches for a stack of books, and throws them at him. Burt ducks, but a hardcover book slices a gash above his right eye. He grimaces in pain and shouts for Cathy to call the Sheriff. This was just one of over 30 run-ins between the two neighbors. Once again, Barbara Ann is arrested and charged with a misdemeanor and is under a 51/50 psychiatric hold at the county jail.

CHAPTER 14

Devil Inside

When Barbara Ann is released she once again stops taking her medication. She wants to be "clearheaded" for the middle school graduation ceremony, which is taking place tonight. It is a joyous event. All the proud parents are snapping pictures of their children, and the school principal gives an eloquent speech, as do several of the students.

When it comes time to hand out the diplomas, it is customary for the school board president to shake hands with the students and give them their diplomas. Well, this protocol makes Barbara Ann angry. How dare she not be able to perform this prestigious ceremonial event.

She leaps onto the stage and demands that she be allowed to make a speech. The crowd boos for her to get off the stage. Barbara Ann pretends not to hear them, makes large gesturing hand movements and shouts gibberish. Just as she does this, the sun's rays expose to the crowd that she is not wearing a bra or underwear. It is not a pretty sight. There was undulating flesh on display to the audience along with stringy armpit and pubic hair. The deeply embarrassed superintendent, Tom, walks up to Barbara Ann and whisks her off the stage quickly.

Humiliated, Barbara Ann marches into the girls' restroom and defaces a bathroom once again. She stuffs way too much toilet paper into the toilet, which causes a river of human excrement and urine to stream out the door and onto the auditorium floor. Children shriek, and the sheriff is called once again to arrest Barbara Ann. As before, she is charged with misdemeanor vandalism, put on a psychiatric hold and released on her own recognizance.

This event makes the newspapers and the local online news outlets. The community is outraged and does not understand how Barbara Ann can stay in office. It is perplexing, but there is a midterm election coming up, so there is hope that another school board member will be elected and rein in Barbara Ann for her two remaining years. The recruitment activity is abuzz trying to find candidates, as three existing board members announce their respective retirements. Friends encourage Jake to run again. He thinks long and hard about this but isn't sure he can make the deadline to file. He is out of town helping to take care of his father, Ron, who is in hospice care at his sister's house.

Jake speaks on the phone at length with Kate, who tells him she will do whatever possible to help him run for office. In fact, she is currently running the family business, which supports them and Ron, while Jake is away from home looking after his dad.

Jake is deep in thought and then speaks to his sleeping, morphine-induced and dying father. "Pop, what do you think about me running again for school board? You know I'm a greenhorn to the community, and I don't know if I can go through the hurt of rejection again."

To his amazement, Ron's eyes open, he stares at Jake and speaks softly, "Son , you're a natural and you must do it—for the children and the community. Stick-'em!"

This makes Jake smile, as he remembers his dad would always shout "Stick-'em" to him before a high school football game, or when Jake had to confront something hard in his adult life. Jake reaches down to his father, gives him a great big hug and kiss on the forehead.

He then mumbles softly, "Pop, what am I going to do when you're gone?"

Jake sees a crooked smile on his father's face and knows his father doesn't have much time. He finds Ron's address book and calls everyone. He puts the telephone on speaker so Ron can hear his family, friends, and colleagues share their favorite memories to say goodbye. They are all going to miss him—especially his son and best friend, Jake.

CHAPTER 15

If You Could See Me Now

After Ron's passing, Jake and his sister work feverishly to bring his body back to the community he lived in for so many years, to be buried next to his beloved wife, Margaret. When the arrangements are made, Jake flies back to his hometown and makes the decision to enter the school board race.

He immediately puts a call into the County Registrar's office to find out how many days he has to make the filing deadline. The woman tells him he has two days. Jake feverishly writes and reworks his Candidate's Statement, reads it out loud to Kate who provides him with wonderful suggestions. He then gathers the necessary signatures and is finally ready before the 5:00 P.M. deadline. He grabs the paperwork, his checkbook to pay the filing fee, kisses Kate on the lips, and heads for the door. As he is stepping outside, he can hear Kate say, "Honey, stick-'em!"

The campaign is on, and Jake works tirelessly by knocking on doors, speaking at candidate events and neighborhood coffees, and hanging campaign signs. He is determined to win. One day, he receives a telephone call from the president of the powerful teachers' union to come in for a meeting regarding their endorsement. Jake accepts but is nervous, because the education system is so different since he last served on a school board over 15 years ago. Nevertheless, Jake goes to the meeting, answers all the questions to the best of his ability, and is appreciative of their courtesy, time, and consideration. That evening, the teacher's union president puts out a press release naming three candidates they endorse for the upcoming election. Two are former teachers, and the third is Jake!

Kate sees this on the online edition of their local newspaper. She lets out a scream and says, "Jake, you got the endorsement!"

Both are floored. The press release includes a statement that the teachers union voted to serve Barbara Ann with a Letter of No Confidence—a stinging rebuke that would undermine her ability to govern or be re-elected. Jake's victory is in the bag!

On election night, Jake and Kate decide not to have a victory party because they do not want to jinx the outcome. Instead, the two of them and their children fly out of state to Kate's father's home. The election returns come in slowly, and Jake is in second place for the three open seats. Throughout the night, he holds on to second place and is victorious. The next morning at breakfast, he tells everybody he has won and is greeted with a hug from his father-in-law, Michael, who says proudly, "Congratulations, Senator Corleone!" Jake smiles back at him and says (in a terrible Marlon Brando impression from *The Godfather* movie), "Grazie, Don Pienza." Everybody laughs at the dining room table and give each other hugs.

At the swearing in ceremony, all the new school board members take their seats at the dais with the remaining board members, including Barbara Ann. The first order of business is to vote who will be the new board president.

Immediately, Barbara Ann nominates herself and there is no second vote. Then another board member nominates Jake, which follows by a second motion. A roll call vote is taken, and Jake is elected president of the district's school board. The overflowing audience bursts into cheers. Jake looks out at the audience and sees Kate's mouth moving and shouting, "Honey, stick-'em!" Jake is on his way!

Chapter 16

Demons

The following day, early in the morning, Tom, the superin-tendent, calls Jake and tells him there is an urgent matter that needs to be dealt with immediately. Jake tells Tom to give him an hour, and he will meet him at his office. Jake arrives, looks around the room and sees the district's lawyer, Ryan, and Tom sitting at a conference table. They tell Jake to close the door and sit down at the table.

Tom proceeds to tell Jake since he is president of the school board, it's his job to "police" Barbara Ann and to see what can be done to remove her from office permanently. Ryan speaks softly and tells them that yesterday Barbara Ann threatened to take her own life and was placed on another psychiatric hold. He then hands Jake a thick manila folder that is labeled "Barbara Ann." Jake takes the folder and starts rifling through it. There are several arrest records, court documents, restraining orders that ban Barbara Ann from the school sites, strange and incoherent writings that look more like a manifesto from a psychotic killer, letters to Tom about people in the community who betrayed her, and on and on. However, the most startling comment was that she wants to kill Jake and is looking to hire a hitman!

The last document in the folder was a ten-page report of an investigation by an independent private investigator, hired by the school district, dated from the prior year. It contained a detailed description of Barbara Ann's illegal and bizarre activities and behavior for the past two years. The last sentence of the report concluded that Barbara Ann "is unable to discharge the important duties of her office due to an unknown mental capacity that severely affects her judgement and behaviors. Therefore, in my opinion, Barbara Ann must resign or be removed from her position immediately."

Jake then exclaims to Tom and Ryan, "Well, this is a slam dunk! We go to a judge with this report and have the investigator testify and then she's gone."

Both Tom and Ryan exchange glances with one another, when Ryan proceeds to speak, "There is one problem, Jake. The investigator died in a mysterious scuba diving accident. However, many eyewitnesses said a green Gremlin was seen driving by the area. Unfortunately, no one could describe the driver or the license plates. This report is now useless. We have no evidence to remove Barbara Ann."

Jake found this incredulous and says, "How can she not be removed from office with all of the arrests? Isn't there something we can do and start a proceeding to have her impeached or boot her out of office?"

Ryan looks at Jake and says, "This type of proceeding is awfully expensive and could be fiscally irresponsible to the school district. The only way an elected official can be removed from office is to have a felony conviction."

Jake bursts out, "What? You've gotta be kidding me!"

As he leaves the meeting, Jake's head is spinning from the information and also also from an unusual case of Ramsay Hunt syndrome, a disease that attacks the ear and trigeminal nerve. The root cause stemmed from Jake's bout of childhood shingles when he was 14, a terrible disease that causes lingering effects. He suffered aches, fever, joint pain, and mild confusion. His symptoms had grown worse after his father died.

However, his crazy crusade to find a way to remove "Batty Barbara Ann" becomes a cause, a mission, an obsession. This helps him focus and keep his thoughts off himself as well as the pain he is feeling. He knows he must complete this task for the safety of his community and especially the children of the school district.

Meanwhile, Barbara Ann is taunting Jake by leaving un-solicited letters, apples, and cards in his mailbox, calling his house and cellphone nonstop late into the evening, and leaving long and rambling messages. She even attempts to kidnap Jake and Kate's beloved family pet, Josie. However, the coup de grace was a Sheriff's Report in this morning's local paper that describes a woman seen with a rifle near their address. Jake and Kate first laugh, and say at the same time, "This craziness must stop—now!"

CHAPTER 17

Obsession

Jake spends hours, which stretches into days, on the internet researching how to remove an elected official from office. He is not having much luck until he comes across a procedure known as a Quo Warranto action. This is a legal action and seemingly proper way to remove Barbara Ann from office. He reports his findings to Tom and Ryan. Both agree this would cost too much money, but they appreciate he brought this idea to them. Jake is flabbergasted. There must be a process in place. After all, Barbara Ann is a threat to the staff, community, and most importantly to the innocent young children of the school district.

Jake speaks with every person in law enforcement he can find, and they all concur that there is nothing he can do until Barbara Ann's behavior escalates and turns violent.

Jake is angry with the system, and says to Kate, "How can someone like Barbara Ann remain as an elected official? What's it going to take, another Columbine, Sandy Hook or Parkland

High School shooting? Kate, I will not quit until she's gone, because under my watch I will not and cannot have any blood on my hands!"

Jake goes back to his laptop and begins digging deeper, and then he finds it. He shouts with glee, "Eureka! Kate, you must hear this. I found exactly what I need!"

He then reads out loud to Kate California Government Code 1770, which states:

"Events causing vacancy in office

"An office becomes vacant on the happening of any of the following events before the expiration of the term:

(a) The death of the incumbent.

(b) An adjudication pursuant to a quo warranto proceeding declaring that the incumbent is physically or mentally incapacitated due to illness, or accident and that there is reasonable cause to believe that the incumbent will not be able to perform the duties of his or her office for the remainder of his or her term."

Jake has his "Ace in the Hole." He says to Kate, "Certainly the California Attorney General will remove Barbara Ann because of this government code. It's clear as day!" Jake writes an email to the attorney general's office.

The following day, he receives an email stating that there is nothing their office can do to help his cause. Next, he writes the governor, lieutenant governor, state board of education, and the superintendent of public instruction. No one responds to his letters except the Executive Director of the State Board of Education. The one paragraph letter states: "The Governor's office forwarded your letter to me for my response to your inquiry. The people have the power to remove an elected official by not voting for them in their reelection." Jake is baffled by this terse response but is not going to give up.

He begins working feverishly to figure out how to protect his community from this monster. A few days later, while sitting at his desk, Gloria, his housekeeper, asks if he has a moment to chat. Jake looks at her and says, "Of course, Gloria. What's on your mind?"

She tells him that Andy, Barbara Ann's ex-boyfriend, is now her live-in boyfriend. Two sheriff officers came to their door and advised her and Andy to be aware that Barbara Ann threatened to kill Andy. This conversation occurred several weeks ago, which was the last time Barbara Ann was arrested for disorderly conduct after refusing to leave a restaurant without a free meal. Jake asks Gloria for the officers' names, and she hands him a business card with a handwritten name. Gloria went even further to tell Jake that Barbara Ann tried to hire a couple of handymen to kill Andy.

Wow, Jake thought, *murder for hire, certainly this will put Barbara Ann away for a long time.*

Jake calls the County District Attorney's office and is told that "saying you're going to kill somebody doesn't provide intent, and we're not going to pursue this matter."

Jake cannot believe this. He needs to clear his mind and somehow wash off the filth and lack of interest by government officials. He jumps into the shower. As he is feeling the warm spray on his face, Kate yells to him, "Jake, you have a telephone call from a reporter from television news."

"What?" yells Jake in a garbled underwater voice. He turns off the water. Kate hands him his cellphone, and he starts speaking to the other voice on the line. The regional area reporter tells him that he has been following this story because of the many newspaper accounts and wants to interview Jake. The reporter tells him he is close to town and would like to meet him. Jake dries off quickly, throws on some clothes, tells Kate about the interview, kisses her on the forehead, and meets the reporter in the local community park.

Chapter 18

Fame

Like Barbara Ann, Jake is subconsciously enjoying the attention he is receiving in the press. He thinks to himself, *Being on television will really provide me with name recognition and further my political ambitions.* His last thought as he leaves his house is, *Gee, Barbara Ann is probably going to make me famous!*

Speaking to a news reporter or leaking information to the press is considered unethical behavior by an elected school board trustee. This type of action could lead to censure, which is a public hearing that leads to embarrassment, rebuke, and typically to the resignation of the disgraced elected official. At this point, Jake does not care what happens to him. The community is insisting he remove Barbara Ann from office at any cost or means necessary. Most of Jake's afternoon is spent chatting with the reporter, telling him the story, his frustration and relaying the lack of caring and courtesy of statewide government officials to even respond to his countless emails and letters. He shows the reporter the letter he received from the State Board of Education. He then gives the reporter a tour of downtown and introduces him to many of the local merchants. All of the small business owners relay the exact same story of how Barbara Ann is banned from their business. They share personal accounts of her bullying personality and disruptive behavior. Jake thinks to himself that this kind of exposure will embarrass the hell out of Barbara Ann, and she will finally resign.

He is wrong. Barbara Ann relishes the attention and even tells the reporter laughingly that she has been placed on several psychiatric holds. Jake's psychologist brother calls this "Good dog, bad dog" behavior, because she seeks attention at any cost whether it is negative or positive. "She's just one sick puppy!" He tells Jake, trying to bring some levity to the situation.

Barbara Ann does not quit her tirade against the community, and her mental state is escalating. She smashes into several cars and flees the scene. Many witnesses testify against her and she is cited with misdemeanors (again), because there is no bodily injury. She just writes another check to the victims and pays for the damages to avoid going to trial.

Several months pass, and Jake attends the state convention of a political party. While he is there, he meets with the Lieutenant Governor and the Superintendent of Public Instruction. Both express concern about Barbara Ann's story, give Jake their business cards and tell him to email them everything he has on Barbara Ann. They promise to look into this outrageous matter and help his cause to have her removed from office. Jake lets out a huge exhale, because he knows this crazy crusade is finally over. When Jake arrives home from the convention, he rifles off several emails and letters to the two elected officials. Weeks go by, and there is no response. He follows up again, and there is no response. He tries calling their offices and is told by office staff they will get back to him. After several months of rejection and no response, Jake is ready to give up on his noble cause. He learns through the statewide political grapevine, he is being ignored because there are not enough partisan votes in his county, and there isn't enough "political capital." This means there aren't enough campaign contributions in his county that will help these politicians beat the other party.

Jake is fed up and exclaims, "Fuckin' rat bastards. All they care about is themselves and their careers. They don't have any desire to help good hardworking folks that pay their salaries!"

CHAPTER 19

300 Violin Orchestra

Barbara Ann decides to run for reelection. Election Day is fast approaching, and she wants to receive Jake's endorsement. She invites Jake and Superintendent Tom to a restaurant just outside of town. There is an unwritten code in town that if a male is going to meet with Barbara Ann, another person must always be present. She has in the past accused several innocent men of sexual harassment. Jake knows many of these people, and investigations were conducted that turned out to be baseless. Neither he nor Tom want to walk down this slippery slope, so they are glad to go together.

After they all finish their meal, Barbara Ann asks Jake for his endorsement. Jake speaks slowly and deliberately to her, "Barbara Ann, in good conscience, I cannot endorse you."

Barbara Ann explodes and hurls a full glass of water at him. Immediately, Jake cautiously wipes his face off with his napkin. Then Barbara Ann begins a tirade about how every man in this town is molesting her, and she has been raped several times in the parking lot of the historic hotel. "The whole community has abandoned me!" She cries.

Jake listens and very emphatically says, "Barbara Ann, I truly feel sorry for you. I really do, but you need to see a counselor or therapist that can help you."

Barbara Ann takes this as an insult and yells at Jake, "You know damn well there are no good psychiatrists or counselors in this county, and I don't need their pity or help."

After her outburst, she starts sobbing. She then shuffles over to the green Gremlin, turns on the ignition and rams into Jake's Mercedes. She then puts the Gremlin into reverse, hits his Mercedes again and drives off. Jake is stunned. Here he is trying to help her, and his effort went south. Fortunately, his car is not severely damaged so he can drive home.

The next day, Jake attends an FBI training course. The topic is how to identify and prevent an active shooter from entering a school campus. He learns that active shooters exhibit the following behaviors and/or traits:

1) Mental health issues
2) Perceived injustice
3) Grievance
4) Bullying
5) Revenge/humiliation
6) Need to regain control
7) Anger
8) Physical aggression
9) Inappropriate firearms use or access to weapons
10) Seeking 15 minutes of fame
11) Physical health changes
12) Tendency to mix alcohol with physician prescribed medication.

After Jake absorbs this information, he sends a text to Kate about what he is learning. She texts back: "Why do you think I have an alarm company installing a central station alarm at our house, especially since there have been a lot of reports that Barbara Ann has been lurking around our home. Besides, everything I ever learned from my years at the FBI is she is going to explode, and it isn't going to be pretty."

In desperation and a last-ditch effort to keep Barbara Ann from being reelected, Jake reaches out to John, a local newspaper reporter, to write a feature and release it before the election. He invites John over to his home. John arrives, and Jake asks him to sit at the dining room table and proceeds to show him his file.

Jake laughs and says, "John, here is your Pulitzer Prize!"

John's eyes widen and look with disbelief at all the information Jake has assembled for him to review.

John reviews each piece of paper methodically and carefully. Every couple of minutes, he breaths out an "Oh, my" or "I can't believe this" or "Why wasn't she put away?"

Jake shrugs his shoulders and says, "Your guess is as good as mine!"

John stands up, gathers all the materials and says he will speak with his editor and write a story before Election Day.

To be reelected, Barbara Ann knows she must deceive voters someway because of the negative publicity she has received over the last several years. She ever so slightly changes the spelling of her last name, and also lists herself as an Incumbent on the ballot. This plan does not work, because the county clerk knows her and knows the correct spelling of her name, so she corrects it for the ballot. Barbara Ann is furious, "You bitch! You are trying to undermine me!" She screams at the clerk as she storms out of the county office building.

Two weeks before the election, the newspaper story comes out. John tries to be unbiased and fair in his reporting, but this article makes Barbara Ann fume with anger. She blames Jake, because he is quoted several times in the piece saying his immediate concern is for the safety of the school staff, community and especially the innocent children of the district. Jake also posts the article on Facebook and other social media avenues.

Jake's strategy works, because Barbara Ann comes in last place in the election. Losing the election causes Barbara Ann to completely lose her mind, and now she is determined to get revenge because of the public humiliation, poor vote count and the dismissal by the community.

On Veterans Day, a local philanthropic women's club is holding a free dinner for all veterans. The meal is lovely, and many speeches are given to honor those who had served their country. The evening turns quiet while the attendees are eating their meal, and Barbara Ann forces her way towards the microphone and asks if she can sing a song. The president of the club gently tells Barbara Ann that she is not on the agenda and to please sit down.

Barbara Ann shouts, "I'm going to kill all of you fucking bitches!" and storms out of the banquet hall. The sheriff is called, takes a report, and dismisses the incident as another "Batty Barbara Ann" episode, but cites it as a "Terrorist Threat." Yet, Barbara Ann is not arrested or cited.

That evening, Jake is returning home from a school board meeting and sees Barbara Ann pass him on the road, honking her horn and screaming, "Get out of my way, asshole!"

Barbara Ann then sideswipes several cars, making the car alarms beep.

Jake follows Barbara Ann to a local gas station and yells, "Barbara Ann, aren't you going to turn yourself in?"

"Jake, get the fuck outta here. You're not the police of me." She screams.

Jake then whispers under his breath, "Oh, yes, I am."

Just then a Highway Patrol officer and several sheriff cars approach. The uniformed officers get out of their vehicles swiftly and move towards Barbara Ann and Jake. One of the officers asks Barbara Ann if she is armed or has any guns or weapons in her car or home.

Barbara Ann says, "No!" Yet she knows she is lying because of her ex-husband's gun collection, which is stored in the basement of her home.

The officer then turns his attention to Jake and says, "Jake, please leave, because you just poked the belly of the beast!"

Jake abruptly leaves, goes home, and tells Kate what transpired. She admonishes him about getting too close to Barbara Ann, and is angry he put himself into such a danger- ous situation.

All Jake can say is, "Kate, I'm on a crazy crusade, and I don't know how it's going to end."

CHAPTER 20

Bang

After the election, several weeks pass and the town is peaceful and quiet. There are no Barbara Ann sightings, and a sense of normalcy returns to the community. The local school board is meeting in Closed Session, and the public is not allowed to participate. Jake is presiding over the meeting when a commotion starts. Someone yells behind the closed doors, "Hey you, you can't go in there!"

Just then, the door to the boardroom flings open, and it is Barbara Ann, nostrils flaring with her favorite red beret ever so slightly tilted to the right. She has come to fight. She pulls a pistol out of her purse and waves it wildly at the dais.

Jake then yells at Barbara Ann, "Put the gun down, now!"

Barbara Ann refuses.

Jake then shouts, "Barbara Ann, this is about you and me. Let the others go—now!"

She reluctantly agrees, and the other board members scurry out and call 911.

Barbara Ann points the gun at Jake and shouts, "Jake, I'm going to blow your fucking brains out and I'll laugh hysterically while doing it!" She laughs manically.

Jake is surprisingly calm and says firmly to Barbara Ann, "Is this how it's going to turn out, your legacy? Do you want your kids and grandchildren to remember you this way?"

Just then a loud explosion can be heard, and a bullet propels towards Jake. The bullet nicks and scratches his right shoulder, and he falls to the floor. He crawls under the dais to try and find a way out. Flashing through his mind is Kate, their children and whether or not he will be alive to see them grow up.

"Barbara Ann, my kids need me, my wife needs me," he screams desperately.

Barbara Ann then yells back at him, "You asshole, you ruined my life, embarrassed and humiliated me in this town. Do I fuckin' care about you? No, I'm going to fuckin' kill you!"

Just then, the doors open and several uniformed officers run in to the room with their guns drawn and yell, "Freeze! Drop the gun—now!"

Barbara Ann slowly starts to turn towards the officers and puts the gun down. She starts sobbing uncontrollably and knows she is going to go jail for a long time.

Jake refuses medical help, places a paper towel on his shoulder and goes home. He tells Kate the whole story, and in a bad English accent he says to Kate, "It's just a flesh wound."

Kate does not think his Monty Python reference is very funny, but is happy he's okay.

Chapter 21

You Oughta Know

Several months pass, and Jake is summoned to appear in court to testify against Barbara Ann. He cannot help but notice how frail and insignificant this bully looks right now. After Jake's testimony, the judge sentences Barbara Ann to two years in jail, and she will have to be under the care of a psychiatrist to ensure she takes her medication. Jake believes this is the end of this chapter in his life.

Jake goes on to run for State Senate, and his number-one issue of his platform is the need for better access to mental healthcare facilities in the district. Jake narrowly loses the election, but he never loses his focus about advocating for a better mental healthcare system.

He shares his story all the way to Washington, D.C., as a passionate advocate. He speaks before members of Congress and to the state assembly. His message is "The System Is Broken." This, of course, is about a failed delivery system and the lack of resources devoted to mental health awareness in the United States, especially in rural California where he lives.

Not even a year goes by, and Barbara Ann is released early from jail for good behavior. She moves back home and runs again for the local school board, which happens to be against Jake for his reelection. On Election Day, somehow Barbara Ann works her way in to the polling place as a volunteer again. She sees Jake and Kate walk in to vote and yells out to them, "Hey, you two, check this out!" She grabs a provisional ballot she believes is a vote for Jake, raises it up in the air, rips it in half and throws it in the trash.

This makes Jake's blood boil. His face changes from bright red to purple, and he starts to charge towards Barbara Ann. Kate knows Jake is in a fit of rage, and this will be a bad situation. Kate runs ahead of Jake and creates a barricade between Jake and Barbara Ann.

She grabs Jake's shoulders, pushes him away from Barbara Ann, and begs him to let go of his anger. She even pleads with him, saying, "Honey, she's not worth it. Let it go, please just let it go."

As she says this, other voters join in and repeat her mantra to Jake. They also grab him to prevent him from going further. Barbara Ann suddenly realizes she has gone too far. She reaches down for a glass of water. However, she grabs a letter opener from the table and lunges at Jake. Just then the sound of gunfire erupts, and several bullets hit Barbara Ann in the heart. It is a kill-shot by an expert marksman—Kate.

Barbara Ann clutches her chest and screams, "Nooo!" A pain that was both sharp and dull spread over her body. Her knees buckle under her and she stops her fall by leaning on a chair.

One of the poll workers screams, "Call an ambulance, is there a doctor or nurse here?"

The many voters in the room reach into their pockets and purses to grab their cellphones and dial 911. Within minutes, paramedics arrive on the scene and start administering CPR on Barbara Ann. It is too late. She's gone. The paramedics then place her lifeless body on a gurney and take her away.

While all the commotion is taking place, Kate looks at Jake and says, "I'm so tired of all of her badgering bullshit, and I had no choice. She was going to kill you! Kate sits down with the sheriff to tell him what happened. Thankfully, there are many witnesses who corroborate her story of self defense against Barbara Ann, a tragic, mad woman.

CHAPTER 22

Unwell

The next day, Jake is in the local post office. Many locals are there, and they congratulate him on his reelection, and ask how is he doing after what happened with Barbara Ann. "I hope Barbara Ann is finally at peace," he says.

There is a deep sense of relief and calm in the town. People are relieved that they do not have to look behind their back or always watch who walks in the door. They can just go about their business and not live in fear anymore.

Jake leaves the Post Office, and a sheriff's car pulls up in front of him. He sees Kate sitting in the back seat of the car. *Uh, oh!* he thinks to himself.

Nick, the local Sheriff, tells him to get in the car. He wants to show them something very disturbing. Jake gets in the car and sits next to Kate. They share an unsettling glance. Nick drives to Barbara Ann's home and invites them into the house. There is a flurry of activity. People in uniforms are scurrying around like rats.

Nick says to Jake and Kate, "Come here, I want to show you something."

They follow him, tripping over the huge stacks of old newspapers on the floor and look inside Barbara Ann's den. Taped on the walls are many faded newspaper clippings about her erratic and bizarre behavior. The first thing they see is a faded newspaper article, which features Margaret's work and effort to create a Historic Walking Tour. Big black letters spell **"SMARTY PANTS!"** across Margaret's face. There are several articles that mention Jake, and a thick black pen circles his name with the words **"YOU'RE DEAD, ASSHOLE!"** There is also a newspaper photo of Jake's proposal to Kate. There is a big black **X** over Kate with the handwritten words scrawled on top of the picture, **"MR. & MRS. PERFECT."** And, next to Kate's photo the following words are apparent: **"I SAW HIM FIRST, BITCH!"**

After taking this all in, Nick speaks up and says, "See, Jake, she not only targeted you, but your whole family. She was obsessed with you and Kate too! Because of this crazy 'shrine' and the fact that she charged you with a letter opener, Kate acted in self-defense, and no charges will be filed. The two of you are free to go."

Both Jake and Kate let out a huge exhale and say simultaneously, "I need a glass of Chardonnay!" They walk hand-in-hand down Main Street to their favorite bistro.

After the server hands them their glass of wine, they toast. Jake says loudly so all of the patrons could hear, "To Barbara Ann, may her tortured soul finally be at peace."

Prior to Barbara Ann's memorial service, Jake is asked by her family to give a eulogy. At first, he resists and is going to decline, but Kate insists he do it. Intuitively, she knows the only way Jake and the community can heal is for him to participate in the service. He reluctantly agrees and takes time to speak with Barbara Ann's family as well as her teaching peers. What Jake discovers is astonishing.

He tells Kate, "It's very unfortunate that I didn't know Barbara Ann before her mental illness spiraled out of control. I only knew the One Mad Apple. Kate, did you know from the time she was a child, she wanted to be an elementary school teacher? She also had a deep love for children, and protecting them was her greatest passion. In fact, if a neighborhood child's parent had to work late, she would take that child in, bake cookies, tell corny jokes, and send them back home, when the parents got home. She also cared for several foster children. I feel honored the family wants me to deliver the eulogy!"

It was a beautiful service, and Barbara Ann's favorite flowers—apple blossoms—fill the church. Many local dignitaries, retired and active teachers, past students, former and current school board members, and almost the entire population of the town show up. Jake greets Jeff (Barbara Ann's ex-husband) and their children.

Jeff leans over to Jake and whispers softly into Jake's ear, "Did you know she was a master gardener? She cherished and loved her apple trees more than anything in the whole world."

Jake and Kate are motioned by an usher to have a seat in the front pew. The minister is very gracious and speaks fondly of Barbara Ann. After she finishes, she asks Jake to come up to say a few words about Barbara Ann's life. Before he starts to speak, he pulls out a small piece of paper out of his coat pocket. He looks at it, pauses, and puts it back.

He then tells the audience "I have something prepared, but I'd rather speak from the heart." He can see some quizzical expressions and has a fleeting thought that everybody is probably thinking he is going to trash Barbara Ann. Jake did not. He speaks eloquently about Barbara Ann's life, her love of family, students, community service, and her deep passion for helping those in need.

After his speech, Jake sits down and begins to weep. First silently, then loudly with his shoulders heaving uncontrollably.

Kate puts her arms around him and says, "Honey, it's okay. Let it go. You need to release all of this. It's the only way it will go away...forever."

Jake agrees. Tears flow down his cheeks and soak his lap.

Kate hands Jake several tissues, and he dries his red, swollen eyes and runny nose. They decide to skip the wake, and as they start to leave, several people pat Jake on the back and tell him how they appreciate how he honored Barbara Ann with respect, dignity and appreciation for her service to the community. Jake smiles, and he and Kate leave the memorial. They both knew this was what Barbara Ann would want. Today, she got it. Jake hoped she could rest in eternal peace.

Two weeks after the memorial, Barbara Ann's house was put on the auction block, sold and razed by the new owner. Everything is gone except for her beloved apple trees.